THE

MW00424176

Jennifer Adams

Illustrations by
Shauna Mooney Kawasaki

Gibbs Smith, Publisher
Salt Lake City

First Edition
08 07 06 05 04   5 4 3 2 1

Published by
Gibbs Smith, Publisher
P.O. Box 667
Layton, Utah 84041

1.800.748.5439 orders
www.gibbs-smith.com

Designed and produced by
  Mary Ellen Thompson, TTA Designs
Printed and bound in China

ISBN 1-58685-451-8

'Twas the Night before Christmas
in Idaho State
And no one suspected
they'd be up quite late,

For back at the North Pole
Nick had gotten some letters
That would have everyone
bundling up in warm sweaters.

"Just look at this, dear,"
said his wife with a sigh,
"We've got letters stacked here
o'er a hundred feet high.

"These letters," she said,
"aren't from good girls and boys
But from mothers instead,
and they're not about toys!

"It seems," she explained
as she sat by his side,
"That there's now a shortage
of potatoes worldwide!

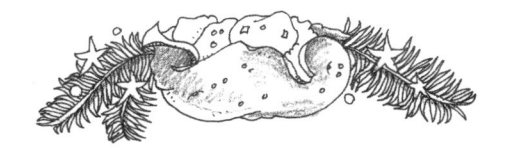

"Without these potatoes
Yule dinners can't be.
It's almost as bad as
not having a tree!

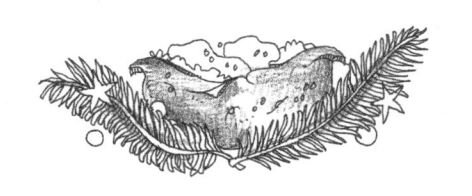

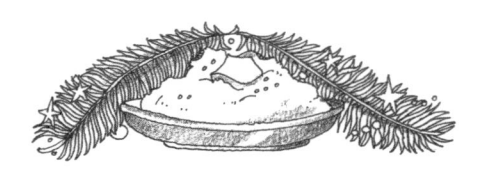

"Think of no baked potatoes,
no Potatoes O'Brien,
No Au Gratin with cheese,
No twice baked, no fryin'!"

"Don't worry, my dear,"
said St. Nick with a wink,
"I know just the answer
without having to think.

"I'll contact my good friends
in Idaho State.
They'll save Christmas dinner—
It's not yet too late!"

So Santa packed early,
and with gifts in his sleigh,
He headed for Idaho
to help save the day.

Sun Valley was first—
lots of tourists and friends
Were there to go skiing
and relax on weekends.

He went to the locals
And told them his plight.
"Not to worry," they said,
"We've got extras all right."

They packed up potatoes
in thick burlap sacks
And gave them to Santa,
who quickly made tracks

To snowy Bear Lake where
he'd stopped by last summer.
The sailing and water-skiing
just couldn't be funner.

The people in condos
would help, he was sure.
They'd give him potatoes
when he knocked on their doors.

Nick headed for Boise
on his Christmas Eve run,
where the wild River Festival
had been so much fun!

When he asked folks for help,
they agreed happily;
As they loaded his sleigh
Santa chuckled with glee.

On Simplot's great hill
all the kids were out sledding.
Their folks gave a ton,
Then Santa was heading

For Boise State U—
now, that's a great school!
Just being a Bronco
is considered quite cool.

The ball team was out
for some Christmas Eve cheer
When they came upon Santa
and his loyal reindeer.

"I have an idea,"
said Santa Claus then.
"Let's have a big contest
and see who will win.

"I'll call up the coach
At Idaho State U
And see if their team
will participate too.

"You'll gather potatoes,
I'll have you on timers.
The team that gets most
will be known as the finer!"

ISU heard the news, and
they shouted, "What fun!
We are the proud Bengals!
Our team's number one!"

They lined up and got ready,
then Santa said, "Go!"
They ran through the town
as it started to snow.

Pocatello's kind people
were glad to oblige,
Giving heaps of potatoes—
Big, small, and mid-sized.

Potatoes soon piled up
All over the town
On porches and rooftops,
Rolling onto the ground.

"Time's up!" Santa yelled.
"Now let's take a tally
Of totals from both teams'
spud-gathering rally."

The reindeer took over
with bullhorns and charts.
They added things up
to see who had best marks.

Then Comet nudged Nick
when the totals were in,
And taking a bullhorn
Nick said with a grin:

"Guess what? It's a tie!
And we counted it right.
Both teams are the winners
this Christmas Eve night!"

He thanked all the players
and townspeople too,
And went on his way.
He had lots more to do.

They flew to state parks.
Winter rangers were there,
And these friendly folks
had potatoes to spare.

Island Park was quite perfect
for some cross-country skiing,
The majestic Sawtooths were
just right for sight-seeing.

To Rexburg and Pineview,
Twin Falls, Henry's Lake,
To Custer's small ghost town—
the full rounds he'd make,

Flying over Hell's Canyon
and Shoshone Falls,
He'd stop by the Snake River,
then take a brief pause

At McCall's winter festival,
now going strong—
Snow sculptures, a dog pull,
people bursting with song.

Coeur d'Alene was a great spot
St. Nick loved to visit—
The landscape so gorgeous,
the shops so exquisite.

In Idaho Falls
people gave even more.
Christmas dinner'd be saved,
Santa now was quite sure.

Bonner's Ferry was next—
such a beautiful place.
Snowmobilers enjoying
the wide-open space.

Santa asked if they had
taters packed in their gear
That they'd share with others
for Christmas this year.

"Why, certainly, Santa,"
each nodded his head.
"We want to make sure
everyone is well fed."

So they pulled out potatoes
they'd saved for their dinner.
"Like you, Nick," they laughed,
"we can always get thinner!"

Nick's heart was so touched by
these people's kind giving,
That a few tears escaped;
he was filled with thanksgiving.

"This state is the Gem State,"
mused Nick, "I know why:
Not cut stones or diamonds
but goodness ranks high!"

But now Santa realized
'twas getting quite late.
"I've got to get going.
I really can't wait."

So he visited houses
from far east to west
Leaving sacks of potatoes
along with the rest

Of the toys and the candy
And gifts for the others,
But he left the potatoes
For all the fine mothers.

The bags went down chimneys
with soft little thuds
Until Santa delivered
each sack full of spuds.

And then he exclaimed
As he drove out of sight,
"Merry Christmas, and thank you
to Idaho. Good night!"